LIFE WITH PEOPLE

A Story

BY

MUFFIT BOW-WOW

(ALIAS DIANE L. BAUMAN)

Illustrations by:

HOLLY A. PLANT

PAW PRINTS PRESS

Sugar Loaf, New York

Library of Congress Catalog Card Number:
89-90777
International Standard Book Number:
0-9622356-0-1

Manufactured in the United States of America

For ordering:

PAW PRINTS PRESS
P.O. Box 386
Sugar Loaf, NY 10981

For my Mother,
without whom, there would
be no story.

This is a true story. It is the story of my life. Once I was very young. Now I've grown old — fourteen years old. A lot has happened to me over the past 14 years — some good, some bad. You might say that my life could be any dog's life, and it often is.

This is a true story. It's a story about sadness and love. It's also a story about fun, responsibility, and the adventure of growing up. It's a story about things that have not been said... Things that couldn't be. It's a story that has never been told until now.

I bury bones a lot better than I write books. There may be times when you do not understand my writing. I will do my best, but I can't forget that there were many times in my life when I did not understand things either.

CHAPTER 1

It's warm. The sun's rays are streaming in through the bedroom window. My fur is touched by the bright, shining warmth; and I groan, stretch, and roll over into a relaxed sleep on my back, feet upward, nothing to do, nothing to worry about. Ho-humm. Asleep on my master's bed, people would see me now and say, "Look at her, she's really leading a dog's life! Not a worry in the world, we should be so lucky!" Beside me lies Missy, Patches, Jesse, and Pete. Pete is curled up on the floor in the one little spot of sun that shines onto the rug. Pete is the oldest dog in our family, and I think that sometimes the warmth from the sun makes his old bones feel better.

I can hear noises coming from the other end of the house. Missy jumps up off of the bed and shakes herself as if to say, "Well, it's time for more important things," The sound of dishes clanging and water running brings the rest of us to our feet. Jesse gives a long, restful stretch. Patches leaps from his warm spot on the pillow and heads for the kitchen. I nuzzle Pete who slowly drags his old body up off the floor. In a moment we have all arrived in the kitchen where our Old Big Person has prepared dinner. Dinner time is such a happy time in our house. The Old Big Person is careful to always measure how much food we are getting so he knows whether he needs to add more or less depending on how fat we are. Sometimes there is very little food in the house, but we always gets our meals and very regularly too. The Old Big Person lines up the five bowls, and we each dive head first into our own bowl. There is really no race to finish the meal because the Old Big Person is very careful to make sure that we each eat from our own bowl. Still it's such a long awaited time of day that we are all sort of in a rush. To tell you the truth, sometimes I eat so fast that I can't even taste the food! At different times in our lives, Patches, Jesse, Missy, Pete and myself have known what it is like to feel hungry. Now, having found the Old Big Person, we no longer worry about starving. The Old Big Person is so good to us that if food were scarce, he would make sure that we all shared the food that was left. At least that is what he tells us. "You are my responsibility now," I've heard him say. "No more suffering for you ever again."

After dinner we all go out for a walk. The Old Big Person usually takes along something to put in his mouth that makes smoke. It doesn't smell good to me, but he seems to like it a lot. Some things about people I will never understand. I guess people just aren't as smart as dogs! This particular night, it was cold in the woods, and

4

we didn't stay out long. The sun was setting, and we could feel the chill of night settling in around our little cabin. The cold night reminded me for a moment of the first cold nights that I spent as a puppy. Pete was the first one back to the house. "Well, friends," said the Old Big Person, "another night is upon us, and it looks like it's going to be a five dog night!" The Old Big Person always said that when it was cold out. We had a fireplace in the main room of the cabin, but the bedroom was mostly kept warm by the five of us lying on top of the Old Man. Dogs have a normal temperature of 102 degrees so you can stay very warm if you have five dogs! "Come over here old man," said the Old Big Person, and he made a bed out of an old blanket for Pete "You've seen the most, and I suspect you haven't much time left." The Old Man gently rested Pete's head in his lap as he crouched beside the old dog in front of the fireplace. "You were my first, Pete 'ol boy. I want you to know that you will always be remembered." He stroked Pete's long black ear as he spoke. "We will be together until the end, and God willing, you will die peacefully in my arms."

CHAPTER 2

I was born in a mud hole under the front porch (No one was expecting a litter of puppies!) It was winter. I once heard someone say that puppies could die outside in winter! Finally, my brothers and sisters, Mom and I (Mom was barely a year old herself and hardly prepared for a family) were moved into something that I later learned was a swimming pool for children! I guess that it was the next best thing to a whelping box. Someone had hung a heating lamp overhead. I loved that lamp. It felt so good to be warm. I used to curl up right under the lamp and go to sleep.

I had four sisters and five brothers. We were all very hungry, and since no one expected Mom to have puppies, she was hungry too and had very little milk. For the next few days we struggled to hang onto a nipple. There were ten of us and only eight working spouts. Food was scarce.

One morning, as I crawled in search of breakfast, I bumped into a cold lump; then another, and another. There was no problem finding an open nipple that morning. Five of my brothers and sisters had died during the night. I did not know why they had died. Maybe they were weaker than the rest of us and couldn't stand the cold and lack of food as long? At the time, I was in the dark about what had happened. (Puppies eyes aren't open for the first ten days, you know!) It's probably a good thing that I couldn't see their stiff, dead bodies. I would have cried and crying with your eyes closed is almost impossible to do. The people in the house seemed upset too. They took my mother away for what seemed like hours. I cuddled with my four remaining siblings under the lamp. When Mom returned we were all frantically hungry. As she walked back into the pool, we attached ourselves to her nipples as though it was our last meal. In a few days Mom seemed to feel much better. I could tell because she licked us more and didn't moan as much as she had before. For the first time we had as much milk as we needed.

When I first saw the world, it was very exciting. BLUE! all around me was blue. (It's not true that dogs are color blind!) The floor was slippery and some spots were wet. It was very hard to walk across the slick, black and white printed floor of the pool. I wobbled and fell down a lot. Each day I grew stronger and finally there was more to eat than just Mom's milk. The food was in bowls. My brothers and sisters and I ate by walking through the bowls of food and spilling most of it. The food was cold and hard to eat without teeth but we did our best.

One day my biggest brother had a terrible experience. He fell into the water bowl! He screamed and struggled for a long time. We all ran over to see what had happened. He splashed cold water all over us. With a final splash, he rolled himself out of the water bowl.

As time went on, the people learned more about raising puppies. They started soaking our food in warm water to make it easier to swallow without teeth. They put our food and water in shallow baking pans which were easier to eat from and much less dangerous. They even put something on the floor to make walking easier for us. With only five of us left and Mom feeling better, we grew fast.

One day, a terribly frightening thing happened. I fell over the blue edge of the world and landed on a cold spot somewhere very far away from Mom and the others. I was so scared; I whimpered and whimpered and finally started to cry very loudly. I was cold, and no matter where I looked, I couldn't see or smell Mom or the family. I trembled for so long that I finally fell asleep on the cold spot.

In a little while I heard Mom sniffing, and I smelled her close by. I scurried towards her and was thrilled to find a familiar nipple. I nursed and nursed until I felt much better. But where were the others?

People came. They picked me up into the air; and before I could see where I was going, I was back with the family. For days this experience upset me. I stayed very close to Mom and cried furiously when she would leave me. I was afraid of the strange world on the far side of the blue.

Soon I was not the only one to have climbed out of the pool into the new world. As we grew, exploring the other side of the blue pool became a game until, finally, the people took the pool away and put us in a puppy pen. At first, living in the pen seemed like a lot of fun. We could see the other world any time we wanted to, even though we couldn't climb out anymore.

After the first few days of being in the puppy pen there wasn't too much new to see, and I got bored. The people fed us four times a day and changed our papers. Mom visited us every few hours (which was my favorite time because we could get to her nipples when she came), but even she was acting as if she was getting tired of us. Once, when I was really enjoying a nipple, Mom reached over and snapped at me. I was confused. I didn't know why Mom didn't want me to eat. She had always licked me lovingly when I sucked milk from her nipple in the past. I decided not to worry about it since I wasn't really hungry. I had four littermates to play with. And boy did we like to play.

"Chewy Face" was my favorite game. I loved to mouth and chew on the faces and ears of my brothers and sisters while they did the same to me. My big brother liked to play "Wolf." That's when you growl and snarl and chase the other puppies through the water pan and all around the pen. When you catch one, you jump on top of him, grab his neck skin in your mouth and shake your head till he squeals. Meanwhile, all of the other puppies pick a partner and wrestle. I did not like to play "Wolf." Whenever I would see the game start, I would hide in the corner of the pen behind a big ball.

We had settled into our daily routine of eating, pooping, sucking nipples and playing "Chewy Face" when strange people came to visit. They didn't feed us, and they didn't change our papers, but I knew they were people just the same. They stayed a long time and put their faces up against the pen. They talked a lot, but I didn't understand the words they said. At first I was very scared. We had never seen strange people outside our pen before. In a few minutes, I started to relax and hesitantly moved around the pen being very careful to keep my eye on the strange people.

All of a sudden I heard a scream and saw my brother, who was bigger than I was, lifted through the air! I quickly ran back to my safe corner behind the big ball and tried to hide. It was a terrible experience. After my brother was taken, all of the other puppies huddled very close together. When Mom returned to us, we nursed for a long time. She licked us more than she had before and seemed to know that one of us was missing. I never saw my big brother again.

A few days later more people came. As soon as I could see them from the pen, I started to shake with fear. Huddled in my corner, I couldn't stop trembling. My little heart was beating faster than I knew it should. My mouth got very dry, but I didn't dare take a drink from the water pan for fear that the strange people would notice me and take me away. Some of the other puppies were walking around the pen. One even jumped up to greet the people. I heard the big people say that I was "shy." I did not know what "shy" was, but I hoped that it meant that I wouldn't disappear like my brother.

The new people had two little people with them. I had never seen little people before. The little people acted very strange. They moved fast and made high, shrieking noises. One of the little people kept looking at me in my corner. I shivered and closed my eyes.

A moment later my most dreaded fear came true. They had chosen me. Of all the friendly puppies, they wanted me, the one hiding for her life behind a big ball in the corner (isn't that always the way life is?)! As they reached into the pen to pick me up, I was so terrified that I piddled all over them. They pretended not to notice a little puppy pee.

One of the people carried me through parts of the house I had never seen. I remember that all of a sudden it got very cold, and then there were strange noises. I could see things moving by very fast, but I had no idea what they were. I started to feel very dizzy. Things were moving by me so fast that I got scared and was shaking. I started to feel sick. Water poured out of my mouth until finally I vomited. The people were not happy about this. For a short time things stopped moving as they wiped my face and paws. But then, as before, things started to whiz by very fast. Finally, I was exhausted and willingly fell asleep in the warmth of the arms that held me.

When I think back to my early puppy days, I realize how silly I was to have been so frightened. But everything was so new all at once. I had never met people other than my own. I had never been around little people. I had never been handled or removed from the safety of my puppy pen. I had never gone anywhere in a big car and there were many strange noises and smells that were new to me. It would have been so much better to have been introduced to the world around me gradually, but my people didn't know anything about raising puppies. They made the innocent mistake of isolating me in a pen for eight weeks and then expected me to deal with a very big, scary world. I'm sure they had no idea of the importance of socializing a very impressionable puppy. I remember being easily frightened by anything new for a long time...even after growing up and becoming a dog!

CHAPTER 3

The next thing I remember is waking up in a box. You're probably wondering, how did I know I was in a box? Well at the time, I didn't, but I knew that I couldn't see anything on all sides of me! From years of experience I now know that when you find yourself in this kind of a mess, you are undoubtedly in a box (at least this is what people call it)!

I did not like being in the box, so I climbed out. Actually, climbed is what I started to do but all of a sudden the box tipped, and I found myself tumbling out into a new world. After a brief shake to regain my senses, I noticed that this new world was warm and quiet. I could smell new smells that I had never been around before. This was truly exciting. As I inhaled a great new smell, I noticed a humming sound. I couldn't tell where it was coming from, and it didn't seem to be too important at the time. The floor of my new world was shiny, hard, and slippery. It reminded me of the black and white paper in the blue pool. I sat in the middle of the floor for quite a while and looked around. Everything was peaceful, and I wasn't at all frightened, which for me is very unusual. Slowly, I made my way towards one of the new smells on the other side of the world. Just as I had regained my balance, it came upon me with a sudden urgency. I squatted and peed for a long time. I felt much better afterward. Feeling quite relieved, I proceeded to investigate the good smelling corners and cracks of the new world.

Just as I started to dig in a corner with very good smells, I heard voices. I couldn't see anyone, but I knew it was voices of people. I started to shiver. Who were they? The next thing I knew, there was a pile of poop on the floor! I had no idea how it got there. I never saw who put it on the floor, but I was careful to avoid it and the wet puddle nearby. I had lots of experience avoiding messes from when I was in the pen with my brothers and sisters. Carefully I found my way back to the box and curled up inside it to rest.

"NO!, NO!, NO!" came the shouts. "You are a BAD PUPPY," one of the people screamed. The yelling was so loud that I started shaking from my head to my tail. I shivered, hid my face and tried to crawl deeper into the box. "BAD DOG," they continued to cry out. I did not know these words, but I did know that there was a good reason to be frightened. "Look," they shouted, "She knows what she's done. She's hiding her face." Actually, I didn't know anything except that I'd rather be somewhere else! "Get out here you bad girl," they screamed as they dragged me out of my box. I was so frightened that my body was stiff, my eyes could see nothing, and my mouth was very dry. The next thing I knew the people were pushing my head into the pile of poop! Why would they do that I wondered. Did they want me to eat it? "Look what you did," they said. I did not know what I had done. I did not know how the pile got on the floor. I never saw it happen. I was very frightened as they continued to scold, and I started to scream frantically. They picked me up, and the next thing I knew I was outside. It was cold outside. They set me down on the outside floor, and I shivered and didn't move. I was too upset to do anything. I hung my head and waited to see what horrible thing would happen next. After a few minutes out in the cold, the people started to talk nicely to me. They even stroked my neck (which was still sore from where they had picked me up). Another trip through the air, and I was back in the box. Boy, was I glad to be back in my box. It wasn't long before my eyes became heavy, and I drifted off to sleep. Just before I fell asleep I remember thinking that the people in the new world didn't like me very much. I wished I was back with my Mom and her people.

I was awakened by a terrible urgency to pee. (If you're paying attention, you'll notice that this happens every time I eat, wake up, or change activities.) Not wanting to mess in my box (which was my only safe, secure place), I jumped out (having perfected the art of not tipping the box), relieved myself and then quickly returned to safety. Before I could even get my paw over the edge of the box, it happened again. The people came running towards me yelling, "BAD DOG! BAD DOG! Look what you did!" they shouted. They picked me up and smacked my bottom. It hurt. I was scared and started to cry. I did *not* know what terrible thing I had done. I did what I had to do. I had always left the area where Mom and I and the other puppies slept, walked across the blue world and relieved myself. Then Mom would clean up the wet spot, and we would all go back to sleep. Why were these new people so angry with me? Why did they yell and frighten me? Why did they hurt me? What had I done that was so terrible? I wasn't happy. In fact, I was most unhappy and very confused!

Before long I was back out in the cold. One of the little people stood next to me. I was so nervous from having been smacked for the first time in my life (which even though short, was all I had to refer to) that I squatted out in the cold. "Oh, Good girl," said the little person and then she patted my head and spoke softly to me. I guess she was feeling badly for what the big people had done to me. The little person carried me inside and placed me on the hard slippery floor. I sat very still. I was afraid that if I started to move the yelling would begin again. The two little people sat on the floor with me. They had a ball (which I remember from my days in the puppy pen) and some other toys that made noises. The little people stroked me and spoke gently to me. Eventually, I relaxed enough to crawl close to the little person with the long, yellow fur. She stroked me until I fell asleep.

It was a short nap. I was awakened to find a meal waiting for me. I'm not sure what it was because it was different from what I had eaten with my bothers and sisters. This food was sticky and different colors. I didn't like it very much, but I was very hungry and ate it all. When I had finished a little person took me outside into the cold. At first I just stood still, but eventually I started smelling the ground and listening to new sounds. After a while I started to shiver, and they took me back where it was warm. The warmth relaxed me, and I squatted and peed.

All of a sudden, the big, angry people who frightened me started yelling again. They yelled at me and at the little person who was holding me. The big people tossed me back out into the cold. This time I was alone. I could hear terrible noises coming from inside. I was cold. I shivered, but in a way I was glad to be missing what was going on inside. I started to walk away from the house and explore the outside. I took time out for a poop and then found a stick to chew on. I was cutting teeth, and it felt good to chew a stick. Before I could get too interested in my stick, the big people came out and picked me up. I arrived back in my box minus one nice stick and things were once again quiet.

Life was much the same for the next few days. I never knew when the people would yell and hit me or why. Sometimes they were nice and held me close and made me feel very good. I was very confused and tried to stay away from them as much as I could. The people put a bone in my box, and I found that chewing on it made my gums feel better. Of course, there was also a blanket in my box to chew, and the box itself was good for teething.

I remember overhearing one of the big people talking to to people I couldn't see. The people they talked to must have been very small because my person held them in her hand and talked to them! My big person kept saying, "She hasn't been housebroken yet." I didn't know what housebreaking was, but I suspected it was something I should have.

I may have never been housebroken if it hadn't been for the good advice my person finally received. They bought me a *dog crate*. The crate was much nicer than my box had been. It was very cozy, and it made me feel safe. It had windows and a door I could see out of! Inside I had a blanket and my toys. It was large enough for me to stand up, turn around and lie down again. I rested very peacefully in the crate, and if I had to get out to pee, I would whine, and the people soon learned that this meant I had to relieve myself. It worked out rather well. The people got trained in less than a day! Whenever I would wake up and not want to soil my bed in the crate, I would cry and instantly they would come running and take me outside. They liked it when I peed outside. From then on there was much less yelling in the house. At night my crate, which was really like a private little room, moved to a different part of the world so my people would hear me if I needed to get out. As I grew older, they even took me and my crate on trips in the car. I could ride safely in the crate with the windows wide open and feel the cool breezes brush against my whiskers. When it was too hot to leave me in a closed car, I sat in my crate with the car windows wide open and waited for my people to come out of a big building. My private room had another use too. If I wanted to get away from the little people (which sometimes happens, you know), I would hide in my crate. It became my own private space in a big, scary world. But best of all, because of my crate, I GOT HOUSEBROKEN!

As time went on I was permitted more and more supervised time out of my little room. This gave me a chance to explore the big house. When I had grown as big as I could get, I started to think of the big house as my house and of my crate as a bed in the big house. I behaved in the big house as I had in my crate and always tried to put pee and poop outside.

Every once in a while, the big people would leave me alone so long that I couldn't control myself, and I had to make a mess in the big house. When this happened, I got very upset. I would pant and pace for hours in front of the door hoping someone would come home and let me out, but finally, I would have to relieve myself on the floor. I hated to do this, and when forced to I always felt very sad. I would hide in my crate until the people came home. When I heard the door open and my people walk into the house, I would shiver and stay in my crate. I never knew if they would beat me or not. Maybe, when they didn't beat me, they knew I had been left alone too long.

The people soon learned that when I did not greet them at the door, it was because there was a puddle on the floor. In time, they also learned how long it was safe to leave me alone. Sometimes other big people would visit me and take me for a walk. When this happened, I was very happy because it meant that I would not have to mess in my house.

CHAPTER 4

I needed to chew. It had become the only thing I thought about. Everything I could find went into my mouth. As I grew new teeth, it felt so good to rub my gums against something hard. In my crate I had a bone and a towel to chew on. Sometimes I even gnawed on the side of the crate. When I was free in the world there were many more things to chew on. Table legs are something you can really sink your teeth into. Did you know that when you chew a table leg long enough, little pieces come off and you can eat them? They don't taste very good, but they are fun to eat just the same.

One day I found a wonderful new toy to chew on. It was a big rug. The biggest rug I had ever seen! I wrestled with it, growled at it, and then lay down and chewed big holes in it. My people were away for a long time that day, and they had left my crate door open so I could play in the big world. Chewing on the big rug kept me busy for a long time. When my people returned home, I greeted them at the door with a piece of the rug in my mouth. I was very proud of my new toy and all the chewing I had done all day. I wagged my tail and carried the piece of rug high in the air to show them what I had done while they were out. I was so happy to see them after such a long time alone.

They were not happy. They yelled and screamed, "My rug! My Oriental rug! Nine hundred dollars in pieces." I didn't understand these words. I didn't know what was wrong. One of the big people started to cry. The other big person, smacked me and smacked me. I was very frightened and started to scream. The little people started to scream too. I tried to run away, but the

big person held me. "BAD, BAD DOG!", he shouted. "How could you do this to us?" Finally, I escaped and ran into a corner in another room. I was very scared and panting very fast. I didn't know how to stop it. Why were the people so angry? Why did they hurt me? Had something bad happened to them while they were away?

The next day my toy was gone. I spent most of the day in my crate. To this day I don't know what an

Oriental Rug is, but I can tell you this: If you ever hear people shouting, "Oriental Rug nine hundred dollars," run and RUN FAST!

After the day I chewed the Oriental Rug, my people put me in my crate with the door closed before they left the house. I liked my crate and really didn't mind sleeping while they were away. After all, there wasn't much else to do except chew my toys. (Puppies aren't allowed to have friends visit or watch T.V. when their people are away, so the next best thing to do is to sleep in your crate.)

CHAPTER 5

"Muffit!, Muffit!" I heard that sound a lot. I soon learned that whenever people said "Muffit" they looked at me. After a while, when I heard the word "Muffit" I looked at them. The people seemed to like it when I looked back at them, and they would talk to me. The words they spoke were often confusing, but I enjoyed the attention.

One day out in the yard I heard, "Muffit, Come!" I had nothing to do and didn't understand what "Come" meant, but I trotted over to the people just the same. One of the people was very pleased with me. She stroked me and played with my face. A little later, I heard it again: "Muffit, Come!" At that particular moment, I was busy smelling a leaf in the grass. It smelled so good that I decided to keep smelling it. All of a sudden a butterfly fluttered by, and I chased it. "Muffit Come!, Muffit Come!" The words were said over and over again. I was busy with my butterfly and paid no attention. The butterfly went up high. I couldn't get up that high, and I lost it. Echoing in the distance I heard, "Muffit, Come!" With no butterfly to play with, I turned and trotted back to the house. As I walked up the steps one of the big people ran out and grabbed me. I shrieked. "You come when I call you," the person shouted. "You are a bad dog. Don't you disobey me!" I cried and struggled, but the person hit me just the same. It was no use. I didn't understand the words "come when I call you." I didn't understand what was wrong or why my person was so mad. All I knew was that I came home to see my people, and when I arrived they grabbed me and hurt me. Finally, the people took me into the house, and I crawled into my crate and slept through the night.

The next day I was again let out into the yard. I smelled the grass and checked to see if the butterfly had returned, but it hadn't. All of a sudden I came upon a smell that was new to me. I started to follow it. Before long I had followed the smell out of the yard and into the woods. The smell got stronger, and I got very excited about where it might lead. Finally, I arrived at a hole in the ground. The smell was inside the hole! I tried to get into the hole to see what had such a wonderful smell, but I was too big (or the hole was too small, I really don't know which). I started to dig, and dig, and dig. After a while there was a very big hole, but when I stuck my head inside, the smell was gone. I closed my eyes and took a long, deep sniff. It was no use. My hole was empty.

While I was digging, it had gotten dark. I was hungry and didn't quite know where I was. I wandered around for a while and then picked up a familiar scent. By following my nose I tracked my way back home.

By now I was really hungry and very tired. I gently scratched on the front door for someone to let me in.

Lights went on, and the people opened the door. The little people were happy to see me. The one with the long, yellow fur knelt down and hugged me. "Muffit, Muffit," she cried, "I'm so glad you came back to us." The big people were not happy with me. They said a lot of words I didn't understand. Something about "property training." The words I did recognize were "Bad Dog!" and "Don't you ever." I knew that these words usually meant I was in trouble. I hung my head and ran to my crate, but I really had no idea why the big people were unhappy with me. I had come home, hadn't I? The big people never came after me, and I was relieved about that. I fell asleep in my crate without a morsel of food for dinner. Somehow I wasn't hungry anymore.

In the morning I ate a big breakfast and was again allowed outside on my own. I played in the yard for a while with a big stick. All of a sudden I heard, "Muffit, COME!" I remembered the sound of those words. The last time I had come to the people who said those words, they had hurt me and yelled at me. "Muffit COME!" they shouted again. I remembered those words well, and I was getting nervous. Would they come after me and hurt me? A big person started walking towards me waving his hand and saying, "Get over here when I call you." I panicked and ran into the woods behind the yard. I ran until the sound of "Muffit Come" was faint in the distance. When I stopped, I was panting very hard. I was very thirsty. I saw a clearing ahead and trotted over to see what it was. The clearing was long. It was easier walking in the open space than it had been in the woods. I started to follow the long clearing. The sun was shining, and the air had a crisp, clean smell to it. I had no idea where I was going or where I was, but it really didn't seem to matter at the time.

Suddenly, I heard a loud rumbling kind of noise. There was also a new smell in the air as the noise came closer. I put my nose high in the air to get a good whiff of the scent. That was the last thing I remember about my trip into the woods behind the yard.

When I awoke my leg hurt badly. I didn't feel I could stand up at all. I was inside where it was warm, and there were voices in the room with me. It sounded like my people and someone else.

"She's a lucky dog," said the new voice. "That car might have killed her. What was she doing on the road? She's a puppy and needs to be protected."

"Yes, Doctor," said one of my people. "We thought she was trained to the property because for the first few days she stayed by the house."

"Property training, as you call it, is unrealistic!" said the doctor. "How can a dog learn a boundary that doesn't exist? Besides, there will often be something that draws a dog off of his property." The doctor continued, "I suggest you put up a fence to teach your pup where the boundary is and to protect her from things that she doesn't understand and might harm her. By the way, why don't you take her to obedience school after the leg heals."

"That's a wonderful idea," said my person. "We'll check into it right away."

CHAPTER **6**

I remember my first day of obedience school as though it was yesterday. I think most dogs remember dog school. Patches and Missy also went to obedience school in their earlier years. Missy described it as a night out when you get cookies for doing silly things. Patches and I talked a lot about our experiences which were, I'm sorry to say, very similar. My people walked with me into a large room. I had never seen so many dogs in one place before. Big ones, little ones, young dogs and old dogs. Most of the dogs seemed as excited as I was. I barked to say hello to everyone and quite a few returned a woof. In fact, there was so much greeting going on that the room was very noisy.

I was standing close to a small, white dog with so much hair in its face that I couldn't tell what it was. I strained on my collar and pulled my people over to sniff noses with the little white dog. I guess I must have caught him by surprise because he returned my greeting with a growl and a snap. Before I knew what had happened, I was fighting for my life. People were screaming and leashes were all tangled up. The little white dog had me by the neck, and I had his paw in my mouth. I growled; he growled and around and around we went. Finally, the instructor came to my rescue and pulled the little terror off of me. Did the instructor call him a terror or a terrier? I'm not quite sure.

My people were very upset. I could sense them trembling, and they didn't smell the same as they usually did. They checked to see that I had no serious injuries. The instructor then calmly made an announcement to the entire class. "Sniffing spreads germs and starts fights,"

28

she explained. "Please keep your dogs away from the other dogs in the class." *Now* she tells them, I thought to myself.

After the fight, the class quickly settled down for the first lesson.

My people had given me a new collar to wear for class. It did not feel good around my neck, especially when it was pulled by the leash. I did not like the new collar. No one had ever asked for my opinion.

My people turned to me and said, "SIT." I had heard that word before in the house. Usually, when my people said "SIT" they had a treat to give me. This night in class there was no treat so I wasn't sure what they wanted. I did nothing. Again my people said, "SIT." Again, I did nothing. Finally, they said "SIT," and I was tired of standing so I sat. "Good Puppy," they responded. I was happy that they thought I should sit when I get tired of standing. So far, dog school was easy. I was sure I was going to enjoy it.

I stood up as my people walked a few steps and again

I heard, "SIT." Since they had said "sit" so many times before, I ignored this first command. All of a sudden they jerked my neck with the collar that I did not like. Then they slapped my rear. Again they yelled, "SIT." The slap hurt me but the collar was so tight around my neck that I couldn't complain. I found myself sitting, but I was very confused. Why had the people suddenly gotten angry with me? Why did they hurt me? I knew what "sit" meant. I would have been happy to have sat, if I had known when they wanted it. The next time I heard "SIT" I was worried and did nothing. I hoped that somehow I could figure this out. Was it the second or third command of "sit" that I was supposed to respond to? Maybe the first? Suddenly they said "SIT!" and jerked my neck before I even had a chance to do anything. Maybe I'm supposed to sit *before* they say it? *As* they say it? By this time I was getting very nervous. No matter how I tried to understand what to do they hurt me with the collar. Feeling helpless and depressed, I hung my head and sat. Maybe the best answer was to *always* sit, I thought.

All of a sudden I heard a new word. "Muffit, HEEL." The next thing I knew, my neck seemed two inches longer and I was jerked up off of the sit (that I thought they wanted) and pulled across the floor. In a few minutes they said, "SIT" and taking no chances, I did. "Good girl," they remarked. "She understands!" they said and seemed pleased. Actually I didn't understand much of anything except to be careful around little white dogs who don't see very well.

Again I heard the new word, "Muffit, HEEL." I sat. They always seemed to like it when I sat. This time they were not pleased. "You stupid dog," they shouted. "HEEL, HEEL!" Now, I didn't understand what "heel" meant in the first place so how was I supposed to understand what "Heel, Heel" meant? Just as before, they jerked me up off of the sit and sent me flying across the floor. OOUCH! the collar stung my neck.

The next time I heard the fateful words, "Muffit, HEEL!" I screamed and pulled back before they could jerk me. I had successfully learned the first night of class that "HEEL" was a warning that my neck was about to be jerked. I also learned that I did not like to "heel." By the end of the first night of obedience school I was exhausted. I slept the entire ride home and most of the next day. During the week my people put the collar I didn't like on my neck a few times and tried to get me to "Sit" and to "Heel." They were not too successful as I did everything I could to avoid being jerked. I pulled away a lot, hung my head, and when all else failed, I would lie down and not get up. After a few minutes of my playing "dead dog" on the floor they would take the collar off, and I would go back to chewing my bones and exploring my world.

In a few days, we returned to class in the big room. I noticed immediately that my little white friend with the hair in his face was not present. In fact, I never did see him again. I certainly wasn't excited any longer about being in class. The thought of having my neck jerked did not thrill me.

"SIT, STAY!" my person commanded. I understand "sit" but "stay" was totally new to me. I thought I remembered my person telling me to "stay there" before leaving the house for a few hours, but I did not know what to do with a "Sit, Stay." I sat for fear of being jerked, but I really didn't know how to please. My person walked around me and then back to my side. I wagged my tail and got up to greet her. "NO! SIT," she shouted. I was now totally confused. I licked my lips and panted. Why didn't she want to be greeted? She had always liked it before. "NO," I understood. That meant trouble. But what did "NO, SIT" mean? I thought that "sit" was what they wanted. After a few more attempts at "SIT, STAY" she seemed pleased with me, but I had no idea why.

We moved to the other side of the large room and again she told me "SIT, STAY." I sat and froze for fear of being snapped. This time there was a long leash attached to my collar. My person walked away, and I started to get nervous. I got up and ran to her. "NO!" she shouted. She dragged me back to the other side of the room and left again. I sat motionless, afraid to make a mistake. The next thing I remembered was being jerked up off of a sit and pulled across the floor. As I started to move, I heard the old familiar phrase, "MUFFIT, COME!" These words had always meant trouble, and it seemed as if things were going from bad to worse.

I was totally confused. I was tired. I was so afraid of being jerked that I finally gave up. There seemed to be no way I was ever going to please my people. Nothing I did prevented my neck from being jerked. I learned to let my

32

mind wander. I thought about sticks and butterflies. I thought about other fun things whenever the people wanted to train me. I resigned myself to being dragged, jerked, slapped, and yelled at with the knowledge that it wouldn't last forever. Eventually we no longer went to dog school. My people called me a "drop-out" and life was once again peaceful. I still cringe when I hear the words "Muffit, HEEL," but I no longer pant or feel sick.

Jesse told me a story about a dog school that he went to that was very different. In this school, the dogs were given a chance to learn what is expected of them before they were corrected for not responding. Jesse said that he really enjoyed learning new words, and he liked being able to understand what his people were saying to him. As Jesse explained, the teachers made it very clear that no dog can be expected to listen until he is taught what to do. The first exercise he learned was how to pay attention, because without that, it's very hard to learn anything else. Jesse said that he was never punished for being confused and only received a jerk when he wasn't paying attention to his owner. "Did you have to wear a special collar that made you feel like you couldn't breath?" I once asked him. "No, all I remember is a round leather collar like the one I used to wear when we went for walks," said Jesse. I wish all dog schools treated dogs with this kind of respect and understanding. I bet there would be a lot fewer dropouts, and the people would have a better time training. I don't think that my people wanted to keep jerking my neck; they just didn't know what else to do. It seems that dog schools can be very different. I wonder if my people ever visited the Dog School before we attended? Were they aware that there are different theories about how to train dogs? I wonder why they didn't sense that they treated me unfairly? I wonder...

CHAPTER 7

"Amy," said Brian, the little person with short, dark fur on his head, "I'm bored. Let's play something." "O.K.," said Amy, the little person with the long blonde fur on her head. "Why don't we play Doctor?" "That's a great idea!" responded Brian. "Muffit can be the sick patient."

The next thing I knew, I was being dragged by my collar into a room where the two little people kept all of their toys. Amy dressed me in one of her doll's tiny shirts. I didn't like wearing the shirt, but every time I struggled to get it off, Amy would yell, "NO MUFFIT!" and slap me on the head.

"Muffit looks so cute," said Amy.

"She's ready to be examined by the doctor now," said Brian. Brian held a flashlight to my eyes and looked in my ears. It didn't hurt, but I would have much preferred chewing a bone or sleeping in my bed. "Nurse Amy," he called, "bring me a stick so that I can check the patient's throat."

"Why do I always have to be the nurse?" complained Amy. "I want to be the doctor this time," she insisted. Amy handed Brian a pencil which he poked down my throat. I choked and gagged and struggled to get away.

"Nurse," he screamed, "hold the patient!"

"Only if I can be the doctor," insisted Amy.

"Oh, all right," agreed Brian. With that, Amy jumped on top of me. "It's no use," said Nurse Brian, "this patient is in pain from a broken leg, that's why we can't hold her." "Nurse, I mean *Doctor* Amy," he continued, "get me some bandages so we can make a cast for the leg." Amy returned with toilet paper and rolls of tape. The little people spent the better part of the afternoon wrapping and taping my legs. The tape stuck to my fur, and it hurt when it pulled the fur. When I was completely covered in bandages, I couldn't stand up. I felt totally helpless and very sad. I did *not* like this game of "Doctor."

The little people carried me all over the house until Brian suggested, "Muffit needs medicine so she can get well." "What can we use for medicine?" asked Doctor Amy.

"Medicine always tastes terrible when Mom gives it to us. What do we have that will taste terrible to Muffit?" questioned Brian.

"I know," shrieked Amy. "Pickle Juice!" Amy ran to the kitchen and returned with a glass of something I had never smelled or tasted before. She and Brian poured the terrible water down my mouth, into my eyes and all over me. I coughed and gagged. Some of the liquid hit my eyes, and I screamed because it hurt so bad. With my legs wrapped in tape I tried to rub my sore eyes. Nothing helped. I continued to whimper. The two little people covered me with a blanket and tried to comfort me. I was tired of the two little people and of their game. As Amy tried to pour more of the water into my mouth. I growled and snapped at her. I had never done that to anyone.

Amy jumped back in fright and ran crying out of the room. "Mommy, Mommy," I heard her say. "Muffit bit me." "Yes," said Brian. "It's true, Muffit growled and tried to bite us." "And what did you do to her?" asked the big person. "NOTHING," said Brian and Amy together. "We were just playing with her."

With the little people out of the room I slowly made my way back to my crate. It took what seemed like hours for me to chew the paper and tape off of my legs. My eyes were still sore from the strange water that the little people poured on me. As I licked the sticky stuff on my legs, one of the big people walked into the room. "MUF-FIT!" she screamed. "What a mess you've made. What did you get into?"

I didn't know all the words she was saying, but I did know that this was not going to be one of my better days. In fact, I was beginning to wonder why I had ever gotten out of my crate.

"Doctor" was not the only game that the little people played with me. Sometimes they would play "Circus Dog." Brian would hold a broom and a chair and make me jump through a hoop Amy held. "Circus Dog" wasn't too bad until I got tired of jumping, and then they would poke me with the broom stick to make me continue to go through the hoop. My favorite game was "Army Dog." The little people would build a wall in front of a doorway. Then they would tie messages to my collar and send me over the wall back and forth between the two armies. "Army Dog" was fun because, when I returned over the wall with the message, they always gave me a cookie for my effort.

I didn't mind playing with the little people. I just wish that there had been someone around to tell them when they did things to me which were unfair or painful. I didn't like to snap or growl, but after a few experiences, I figured out that it was an easy way to tell the little people that I didn't want to play anymore. The big people did not like it when I growled at Amy or Brian. Once they even talked about getting rid of me. They said that they thought I might be "turning on them." I wonder what they thought I was turning into? Lucky for me that soon after our last game of "Doctor" the little people lost interest in me and hardly ever wanted to play anymore. In fact, it wasn't long before the little people did not want to do anything with me anymore. They never walked me. They never brushed me. Sometimes they would forget to feed me. I learned to rely on the big people for anything I needed.

Missy had little people in her family too. She used to tell us about her little person named Suzy. Suzy was always very gentle with Missy. She brushed her coat, cleaned her ears and took her for long walks. "Suzy always took very good care of me," said Missy. "Once I was very sick and Suzy stayed with me all of the time. She even cooked special food for me that wouldn't make my stomach ache. I always felt safe when Suzy was home. I slept on her bed every night and all I had to do was look at her in a special way, and she would know that I needed to take a walk." Some little people can be very responsible with dogs. Who teaches the little people about caring for dogs? It must be the Big People I thought. And whom do they learn from?

CHAPTER 8

I was almost a year old. I could tell because the little people were planning a birthday party for me and they kept saying, "Muffit will be one year old." I didn't know what a birthday party was, but I hoped that it would be fun.

During the days before the party, I did not feel very well. In fact, I felt very strange. My stomach hurt, and sometimes I didn't even feel like eating. I was very tired and not even interested in chasing butterflies and good smells. I slept almost all day for quite a few days. No one but me seemed to notice.

The day of the party I felt quite a bit better but noticed early that morning that a part of my body was changing. I smelled different and wanted to lick my bottom a lot.

At the birthday party each of the little people gave me a new toy. Brian gave me a great big chew bone, and Amy gave me a ball that made a noise when it rolled. Instead of my usual breakfast, the big person made what she called, a "cake," out of meat and cheese. I was very pleased with the food and toys and wondered why I couldn't have a birthday party every day.

After the party, which to my way of thinking was much too short, the little people went outside, and I returned to my bed to sleep and chew my new bone.

For the next few days I continued to lick myself a lot but paid less attention to why my bottom was getting larger.

That afternoon the big person tied me to a tree outside where I often spent a sunny afternoon. The people never did put up a fence like the doctor had suggested after my car accident. Actually, I didn't mind being tied to the tree too much except when I got tangled up in the rope. On this particular afternoon, I had lots of visitors! Dogs from all over the neighborhood that I had never seen before were coming to sniff me and try to play with me. They all seemed very friendly to me, but two of them got into a fight with each other. The fight caused a lot of noise, and my big person came out and took me back inside the house.

The next day I was again tied to my tree when a very big, black dog came to visit. He licked my ears and danced around me making little whining noises. He also licked my bottom, and it made me want to stand very still. All of a sudden, the big black dog jumped on top of me. I was frightened as this had never happened before. Some feeling inside told me to stand up straight and lift my rear to him. I felt a sudden new feeling and just as I started to

relax, the dog got off. He tried to pull away, but he couldn't. We were stuck together! Just then, one of my big people walked outside. "OH!, NO!" she screamed. "Muffit's been bred." I did not know what "being bred" meant, but in the weeks that followed, I was to find out.

CHAPTER 9

A few weeks after the "breeding" my people took me to the doctor who had helped me when the big car had hurt me.

"It sure looks like she's pregnant," said the doctor. "When did this happen?"

"Three weeks ago," said my person.

"Three weeks ago! You should have brought her in right away, and we could have given her an injection to avoid this pregnancy," he explained.

"We didn't know that such a shot was possible," said my person. "We had hoped she wouldn't become pregnant since it was only her first time," explained the big person.

"Do you know she is going to come into season about every six months? Each season will last twenty one days," the Doctor said. "In fact," he continued, "during the heat cycle she can be bred by numerous dogs and deliver puppies in the same litter with different fathers."

"I didn't know that," said one of the big people. "How will we know when she comes into heat again?"

"There are definite signs if you look for them," explained the doctor. "The female dog's vulva will swell, and she will begin to show a bloody discharge. After a few days, the discharge will become a light pink color. It is at this time that the female dog, or "bitch," is usually anxious to breed and most likely to become pregnant. You may even notice some changes in the female's behavior as she comes into heat. Some female dogs get very tired, and it is not uncommon for them to refuse to eat for a few days."

"Now that Muffit is pregnant what can we do?" asked one of my big people.

"Well," said the doctor, "we can either let her have the litter or spay her now and abort the unborn puppies. She should have been spayed before she ever came into heat. It would have been a lot easier and is much safer surgery."

"Do we have time to think about this?" asked the other big person who was with me.

"Decide by the end of this week if you want to spay her. Make an appointment with my nurse for next week," replied the doctor. As he turned to leave, the doctor muttered, "Poor Dog!"

The next few days, there was a lot of talking in the house. Almost every other word was "MUFFIT" and this concerned me. I had no idea what I had done. The little people cried a lot and hugged me more than they ever had before. I heard them say, "Poor, poor Muffit. You will never be a Mommy." I knew something was wrong, but I had no idea how to fix it. "What's a Mommy?" I wondered.

We all made another trip to the doctor. One of my big people handed me to a strange big person who took me to a big dark crate I had never been in before. I could not see my people. I could not hear my people. I started to get very scared. I cried and barked but no one came to see what was wrong. I tried to bite the bars of the crate but they were too strong. "Was this the end?" I wondered. "Were they going to leave me and never come back? What terrible thing was going to happen to me?" I was panting so hard there was a puddle of water just under my tongue when the nurse came in to visit me. "You poor thing," she said sympathetically. "What did they let happen to you?" she said and gently stroked my head. Looking into my big brown eyes she smiled and whispered, "Everything is going to be all right. You don't need to be so upset. You will go to sleep for a little while and when you wake up all of your problems will be over." I didn't quite understand what she was saying but her tone of voice was so sweet and gentle that I started to relax and laid down in the crate.

The doctor came to visit me and gave me a very tiny shot. So small that I could hardly feel it. All of a sudden I felt very, very tired and closed my eyes. I drifted off into a quiet, peaceful sleep.

The next thing I remembered was waking up in the crate and feeling very sleepy. A big person offered me some water, but I was too tired to drink. I laid my head back down and fell asleep. A few hours later I did awaken and have a drink. My stomach felt a little sore but nothing so terrible that I couldn't drift back to sleep. That's how my day went. I would wake up briefly and then drift back to sleep. In the evening, I had a small meal and went out for a slow walk. I slept the whole night through and didn't even think or worry about my people. I just wanted to rest.

The next morning I was feeling much better and ready to get out of the crate. To my surprise, my people were waiting for me in the office. I could hear their voices and the doctor talking to them.

"Now, she has just had surgery," said the doctor. "Since she is a dog, she doesn't know this, and you will have to keep her quiet. She is not in much pain and will probably want to run around, but don't let her. She needs to be kept quiet for a few days. No running or jumping. These stitches will dissolve so you don't need to bring her back. Give me a call if you have any problems." A big person led me on a leash into the waiting room, and I immediately ran to greet my people. I had no idea what had happened over the last two days, but I was glad that it all seemed to be over.

In the car on the ride home I heard my people

talking. "If I had realized how simple it was going to be to have Muffit spayed, I would have arranged to do it much sooner," said one of the big people.

"I know," replied the other. "I just wish I had noticed when she came into heat," said a big person.

"What's a heat?" asked Brian.

"Nothing you need to worry about," said the big person.

"What about me?" questioned Amy.

The two big people just looked at each other. No one answered Amy's question.

CHAPTER 10

The two big people and the two little people were sitting around the table having a meal one morning. As usual, I was curled up under the table waiting for any small crumb of food that might come my way. Amy's spot at the table usually provided the best morsels but as the years had passed, and the little people grew up, I noticed that less and less food made it into my mouth under the table.

There was a time in my life when the big people would feed me anything and everything that was left over on their plates. At first I really looked forward to these treats, but after getting sick over and over again from spaghetti sauce and other spicy foods, my people finally learned that what they saved in dog food, they spent on trips to the doctor. Now they feed me only my special food. It's the same food every morning and evening. I like it that way because I always know what to look forward to.

There are times when I don't feel like eating because my stomach feels funny. My people used to worry about me and offered me treats to coax me to eat. They soon realized that when I didn't feel good, the treats would make me sick. Now the people have learned that if I choose not to eat my food, they should not offer me something more tasty. My stomach always lets me know if I should eat or not.

It was while I was under the table waiting for crumbs that I overheard the people talking about me.

"Muffit is such a good dog," said one of the big people.

"Yes, you are right," agreed the other.

"She never does anything wrong," added Amy.

"David's dog always runs away and chews up his sneakers," said Brian.

I was in shock. Had they forgotten about my trips into the woods? Had the Oriental Rug slipped their mind? What about the time I growled and snapped at Amy? It all seemed very strange to me that they had forgotten all about my exciting puppyhood. I had not forgotten all the times they hit me when I didn't understand why.

After puppyhood, the years had passed very quickly. I learned the routine of the house, and my people became trained. Before I realized it, I was eight years old.

Finally, I had taught my people how to raise a puppy. Now all they can remember is how wonderful things have always been. I don't know if I will ever understand big people or little people.

"Since Muffit is so wonderful," said Amy, "couldn't we get another puppy to keep her company?"

"Oh, yes," added Brian, "we haven't had a puppy in such a long time."

"Well, I don't know," said one of the big people. "You children will be going off to school soon and then it will just be your father and me left home with the dogs," said one of the big people.

"I don't see why not," said the other big person. "Charlie, down at the plant just had a litter of "Pedigree" Irish Setters. Let me talk to him today."

"George, are you sure we need another dog?" asked the other big person. "The children hardly pay attention to Muffit as it is," she continued.

"I kind of like the idea of having a hunting dog," said George. "Let me talk to Charlie about the litter. They're probably all sold anyway," he added.

As I chewed a piece of toast that had finally reached the floor, I wondered what was so special about a "pedigree" Irish Setter. I have a pedigree too, I thought. All dogs do! A pedigree is a list of your parents and their parents. My pedigree is as long as any other dog's is. Why if they have a pedigree Muffit do they need another dog? I'm not sure I want to deal with a puppy at my age. Who do they think is going to have to raise it?

My life had settled into a very pleasant routine. I had become a very happy, lazy, pet dog. About the most exciting thing to happen recently was when my people went on vacation and left me at the Doctor's. I wasn't sick when they left so I don't know why they left me there. I sure was sick when they came back to get me. I coughed and coughed for weeks. Since then, whenever they go away and can't take me, they leave me at a kennel with other healthy dogs whose people are away. I don't know where people go on vacation, but for me, the kennel is a vacation from them, and I really have a good time barking and running with other dogs.

The meal ended. My people left the house, and I curled up in my crate for a sleepy morning. I thought about what my pedigree would look like if anyone ever wrote it down. I bet it would be very long.

My peace was not to last much longer. That evening I met a "Pedigree Irish Setter."

CHAPTER 11

"Brandy" (that must be a common name for Irish Setters, because I have met many "Brandys" in my short lifetime!) was placed on the shiny floor in front of me. At first I just watched him scamper about the kitchen. "Look," said Amy, "He's just the 'cutest thing' the way he can't seem to get his feet under him when he runs."

"Yes," said a big person. "he's very cute but seems to have an inexhaustible amount of energy. He hasn't stopped running since your father brought him home."

Brandy stopped running just long enough for me to get a sniff of his rear.

"Ooucch!," I screamed. Brandy has just sunk his sharp little baby teeth into my tail and was hanging on. I quickly turned around and growled at him to let go. "NO MUFFIT!" shrieked one of the big people. "You leave the baby alone," she ordered. Before another word could be said, Brandy had taken hold of my leg and was shaking it. I reacted and jumped on top of him, snapping as I went. I was not a play thing, and it was time for Brandy, the "cute thing," to find his place in the order of this family. I was here first!

"Help!" screamed Amy. "Muffit is attacking the puppy!" The two big people stormed into the kitchen. Before I realized what had happened, Brandy and I were on opposite sides of the room.

"BAD, BAD DOG!" shouted one of the big people into my face. "I don't understand why you would attack a puppy. What has gotten into you?"

They didn't understand and neither did I. Life had been so peaceful. There had been very little shouting

until Brandy came. Why did they wait till I was eight years old to bring a red terror into my life?

Brandy and I never became the best of friends, although he did learn not to sink his teeth into me. Aside from all the attention that Brandy received that should have been mine, what upset me most of all was the day that they gave Brandy *my crate!* "Muffit," they said one day, "you can sleep on the floor now because you are all grown up. Baby Brandy needs to sleep in the crate." I was horrified. This was my private, little room. It had all my smells in it. It was my security and besides, I liked my crate and didn't want to give it up. Whenever I would pass by the crate and see Brandy sleeping in it. I would give a low growl. I just wanted him to know that it was my crate he was sleeping in.

They bought Brandy all new toys that made squeaky noises. I liked the toys, but whenever I would take one to play with, the little people (who were starting to look more like big people every day) would always take it away from me and say, "No, Muffit, this is Brandy's toy." I didn't understand. If he could sleep in my crate, why couldn't I play with his toys? Actually, there was a lot about Brandy that I didn't understand. He was always running. He very rarely slept and barely ate his food. I found this behavior very strange, but then, what did I know about a "Pedigree Irish Setter."

Brandy grew very big. Before he was one year old he was much bigger than me. When he would run through the house, he would often knock things over and cause a lot of confusion. As Brandy grew out of puppyhood, he got into more and more trouble. The people shouted "NO" at him a lot. Brandy liked to jump up and put his paws up on the big people. When this happened, the big people would yell "NO!" and lift their knee into him. Brandy didn't seem to care. He would run around behind them and jump up on their backs! One day the big people learned a trick. When Brandy put his paws up on them, they took hold of his paws in their hands. "You're such a good boy," I heard them say to him. "I'm so glad you like to greet us," said the big person to Brandy who was still standing on his hind legs with his feet stuck in the big person's hands. Every time Brandy would jump on the people, they would grab his paws and say sweet things to him. Brandy was big, energetic, but not stupid. He soon learned that if he put his paws on people he might not get them back! It was only a few days after the people learned the trick that I noticed Brandy had given up the idea of greeting people with his feet. I kept waiting for the day when Brandy would go to obedience school. I was sure that his manners could be improved with some education. I waited and waited, but Brandy never went to obedience school.

One day some men came to the house and put up a fence. From that day on, Brandy lived in his own little house outside. I was also allowed outside to run around with him, but most of the time I would just stand by the door and ask to be let back in. With Brandy outside, the quiet peacefulness of the house returned. And the best part of it all was that I got my crate back!

Sometimes I felt sorry for Brandy outside in the cold. In the winter his water would freeze and he would have to lick ice instead of drink. His house had no door or bedding inside of it and I know that it had to be very cold when the wind blew.

One day Brandy caught his chain collar on the fence. He was stuck and choking! I could see him from the window and I barked and barked. The big people came to see what I was barking at and when they saw Brandy hanging on the fence, they were very upset. They rescued him and removed the dangerous collar from his neck. After the chain collar scare, Brandy was given a new leather buckle collar to wear. Because it was loose enough to slip out of, if it got caught on anything we didn't have to worry any more about Brandy hanging himself. I guess you could say that I saved Brandy's life. If I hadn't seen him hang himself on the fence, he might have died.

CHAPTER 12

When Brandy was five years old, I was thirteen. He was still running around the back yard as fast as ever, but I could feel my old body slowing down. While I still had thoughts of chasing butterflies and walking in the woods, I usually felt like sleeping. On the cold winter mornings, it became harder and harder for me to drag my old bones outside into the cold to relieve myself. Sometimes I would be sleeping so soundly that I wouldn't even wake up and would pee in my sleep. This was very upsetting to me.

It had been a long, snowy winter and spring was just starting to show its face. The grass was turning green and smelled very sweet and new. In the early morning I could hear the familiar sounds of birds chirping. I was excited because I knew that soon there would be butterflies to chase and a strong warm sun to snooze in.

The big people and the little people had been doing a lot of talking. I was too busy sleeping to understand much of what they said, but I did overhear words like "country" and "back to nature." I had no idea what it all meant, but after thirteen years of living with these people I had learned to expect almost anything.

The next day, the two big people and the two little people and I all went for a long ride. It was a clear, crisp day, the kind that makes you eager to run in a field and chase rabbits.

It was a very pleasant surprise to me when we arrived at a huge field in the country. I had never been to such a wonderful place before and was very excited. We all got out of the car, and the little people threw a ball for me to play with. I ran like a puppy through the high grass in the field. Amy and Brian cheered as I returned the ball to them each time. When we were tired of playing, the people sat on a blanket in the grass, and I laid next to them.

"Muffit has been such a good dog," said Amy almost tearfully. Then she stroked my back and nibbled a sandwich. "Why can't we keep her until she dies? I don't understand why she has to leave us now," questioned Brian.

"Muffit is too old to live in our house anymore," explained one of the big people. "She is starting to have accidents in the house and will probably die soon anyway. It's best that we return her to nature and give her back her freedom to do what she wants to with her last remaining time," said the big person.

"But who will care for Muffit?" asked Amy. "Who will feed her?"

"You don't need to worry about Muffit," explained

the big person. "Dogs can take care of themselves. Muffit will learn to hunt for her food and live in a cave. She will return to the wild instincts of her ancestors."

"I've never seen Muffit ever hunt for anything," said Brian suspiciously. "I bet she starves out here in the country. She may even get attacked by wild dogs who don't know her! I can't believe that you are really going to leave Muffit out here to die!" said Brian in an angry tone.

"You don't understand," said the big person calmly. Then she continued, "We cannot keep a dog in the house who can no longer stay clean."

"Jenny's family put their dog to sleep when it got too old," said Amy. "Amy!" shrieked the big person, "How can you even think of such a thing. Are you suggesting that we kill Muffit?"

"I wasn't thinking of it exactly that way," said Amy softly.

Brian looked at Amy. Amy looked at Brian. Then they all looked at me. "Get in the car," said the big person.

I did not understand what the people said. I was very happy lying on the blanket in the sun and eating bites of sandwiches that Amy fed me. "Why don't we do this more often," I thought.

It was a lovely day. The little people played with me more than they had in a long time. I chased the ball and sticks and rolled in the high grass with Amy and Brian. Amy hugged and kissed me. I was so happy to be out with the family alone (we had left Brandy at home!).

As the sun went down the big people loaded everything back into the car. Then a very strange thing happened. I started to jump into the back seat to ride with the little people, when one of the big people gently pushed me aside and said, "No Muffit. You stay here. Run with the wild dogs and enjoy your freedom. We love you but you can't come home with us this time." Then they all got into the car and drove away. I could hear Amy and Brian yelling, "Good-bye Muffit." I stood in the field for a moment and then took off after the car. I could not believe that they had left me behind! I did not understand. This had to be a mistake! I ran as fast as I could but it was no use. In a matter of moments the car was out of sight and I was out of breath.

I collapsed flat out on my side breathing very heavily. Why? Why did the big people and the little people leave me in the field? What was all this talk about being free and running with wild dogs. I didn't know any wild dogs. When I caught my breath, I found a soft mound of leaves left over from the fall and curled up to lick my feet which were sore from running so fast on the road after the car. They'll come back I said to myself. I know they will. They have never left me before and not returned.

It got dark, and it got cold. I went back to the field where Brian, Amy, and I and the big people had laid on the blanket. I could still smell them in the grass. I curled up and tried to sleep. There were many new sounds in the country. I felt very alone and frightened. "I will wait for them to come back," I said to myself over and over. Finally I drifted off to sleep.

CHAPTER **13**

I awoke very early. It was cold and damp out in the field. My body ached, and I was very stiff from the exercise the day before and having slept outside all night. I was used to a warm crate with a blanket, not a damp, cold field.

I was hungry, and I had a funny feeling that I was not going to find a bowl with my favorite food in it this morning. I wandered around the field smelling for something to eat. As I moved a bit, my bones seemed to work a little better. As the years had passed, my eyes had gotten worse, and I had learned to rely on my nose more and more. Actually, it's not really a problem because dogs have a very good sense of smell. I chewed on some grass but found nothing that resembled real food.

That afternoon I stumbled across a stream with running water. I was very thirsty and decided after I took a drink that I should stay close to the stream.

Nothing much happened for the next two or three days. I'm not really sure how long I was in the woods by the stream, because after a while I was so hungry I didn't feel very good. I slept and slept and couldn't concentrate on anything. I would wake up feeling cold and hungry and then fall back to sleep. It rained the day after my people had left me. My wet coat made it hard for me to get comfortable or warm even when the sun finally returned.

I probably would have died out in that field, but as you already know, I didn't. I'm sure you've figured out by now that it was the Old Big Person who saved me.

I remember waking up on a soft blanket in a warm place. The Old Big Person was sitting beside me and

gently stroking my head. "You poor thing," he muttered. "They abandoned you like they do to so many old dogs. It's so unfair. They really don't mean to be cruel. They are just ignorant. They don't realize that a dog who has lived its whole life as a house pet cannot survive in the wild. Don't worry," he said, "you can live out your remaining time with me and Pete and Missy and Jesse and Patches. I found them much the same way I found you," and he stroked my head again. "What's your name?" he asked. I sighed and moved my head closer to the hand that stroked me.

"No matter," said the Old Big Person. "To us you

will be called Lady. I bet you've always been a little lady all your life." I did not know the words that the Old Big Person used, but they sounded sweet and comforting and I liked it when he spoke to me.

As I woke up, I could see and smell the other dogs around me. They sat very still and then one of them sniffed me as if to say, "Hello, welcome to our family."

The Old Big Person, Patches, Jesse, Missy, Pete and I all live together now in the cabin in the woods. We are a family. We take a lot of walks in the fields nearby, and every one of us takes care of each other. Shortly after I arrived, Pete was ill, and we all stayed very close to him to keep him warm at night. The house we live in has a small fire in it, a table and a small bed for the Old Big Person. All the dogs sleep on top of the Old Big Person at night or under the bed on a blanket. Pete is better now and is back to chewing on sticks, which is his favorite thing to do.

I still think about my other family. I wonder how Amy and Brian are growing up. Sometimes I even imagine that Brandy is allowed back in the house as he becomes an old dog. I still don't understand how a family could give up a dog that lived thirteen years of her life with them. I don't think I will ever understand.

I've been lying on the Old Big Person's bed in the sun writing my story for the past few days. I'm glad I got the chance to tell you about my life. I know that Pete, Jesse, Missy and Patches all enjoyed listening to my story. I'm feeling very, very tired now. I can't ever remember feeling this tired or this content before. I need to sleep. Thanks for listening. By the way, if you own a dog, be good to him, and tell him that Muffit says, "Hello."

THE END?